ROY APPS
DEADLY TALES

The Party
Animal

and

Don't Look
Under
the Bed

First published in 2012
by Franklin Watts

Text © Roy Apps 2012
Illustrations by Ollie Cuthbertson © Franklin Watts 2012
Cover design by Jonathan Hair
and Peter Scoulding

Franklin Watts
338 Euston Road
London NW1 3BH

Franklin Watts Australia
Level 17/207 Kent Street
Sydney, NSW 2000

A CIP catalogue record for this book
is available from the British Library.

ISBN: 978 1 4451 0338 9

1 3 5 7 9 10 8 6 4 2

Printed in Great Britain

Franklin Watts is a division of Hachette Children's Books,
an Hachette UK company.
www.hachette.co.uk

CONTENTS

The Party Animal

Don't Look Under the Bed

The Party Animal

1
Betrayal

Mia, my darling older sister. I hated her.
Charlie had been *my* boyfriend until she
stuck her great ugly face in. OK, we'd only
been out a couple of times – once shopping
and once to see a movie – but he really liked
me, I could tell. That was until I invited him
home and he clapped eyes on her. Mia. Next
thing I knew, Charlie was taking her out; to
pubs, clubs, the lot.

And then, the worst thing of all! Mum and
Dad went away for the weekend. So Mia
decided to have a party – with Charlie, of
course – at our house!

"Oh, for goodness' sake, Nadia, grow up,"

Mia told me. "I can't see what your problem is, I really can't."

"You're the problem," I snapped. "You, and him!"

"Look, you can either come to the party tonight, or you can stay in your room and sulk like the saddo you are," Mia replied.

Well, there was no way I was going to hang about downstairs, watching Charlie and Mia paw each other all evening. I sat in my room, watching a rubbish horror movie. From downstairs came the constant thud-thud of dance music. About twelve people had turned up – Mia hadn't advertised the party on her Facebook page – but what with the squeals and laughter, there was enough racket to wake every zombie in town.

Suddenly, above the sound of the party, there came a sickening screech of car brakes.

I looked out of the window and saw a bright red car race away. What was all that about? I thought. Then I realised I was starving and the only food in the house was downstairs.

Luckily, they'd left all the food in the kitchen. Mia knew that Mum would go mad if she came home and found the carpet had leftover bits of food squashed into it.

There were crisps and stuff, and I saw that Mia had put out the beef that Mum had put in the fridge for our sandwiches. There was hardly any left! I was grabbing the last slices, when I heard whimpering at the back door. Jasper, our pet dog, had been shut outside! I bet no one at the snog-fest had even thought of feeding poor Jasper.

I opened the back door. I knew straight away that something was wrong. He seemed to be limping. I threw a few pieces of beef into his bowl. He staggered up to it, sicked up on the floor, then he toppled over wheezing like mad. What the…! I bent down to stroke his back, murmuring gently to him, while he groaned. Suddenly, his head lolled over onto the floor and he was completely still. Jasper! I shook him, but he was gone. Tears welled up in my eyes.

Slowly, a smile crept across my face. I knew what I had to do.

2

Tragedy

In the lounge, Mia and Charlie were in such a close clinch, it would have taken a team of skilled doctors hours to separate them. The lovers didn't see me, of course.

I strode up to Mia and shouted in her ear — the one that wasn't being nuzzled by Charlie: "Mia!"

Mia and Charlie sprang apart as if I'd just put about a million volts of electricity through them.

"Nadia! You little —"

"Jasper's dead!" I said. Mia looked hard at me, and saw the tears in my eyes.

They all followed me through to the kitchen. Mia gasped and put her hand to her mouth.

"What happened?" asked Charlie, swallowing hard.

I shrugged. "He was eating his supper, then he staggered and he was sick. Then he just kind of fell over…" I couldn't stop the tears rolling down my cheeks. I was actually upset, after all.

It was Mia, clever Mia, who tumbled to it first of all. "You gave him some of that beef, Nadia?"

I nodded. "Well, there wasn't much left and…"

Mia started swaying about rather dizzily, "I don't feel well…"

Now it was my turn to put my hand up to my mouth in horror. "You don't think it was the beef…?"

"Jasper ate the beef. Jasper was sick. Jasper is dead. I ate the beef…"

"Do you feel sick, Mia?" I asked, innocently.

Mia nodded, fearfully.

I frowned. "I suppose that beef had been around for quite a while," I said deliberately.

Some of the others started muttering: "Oh no! I had some of the beef, too!"

Everyone's eyes were on poor, dead Jasper, lying in a pool of sick. Mia was sobbing, more from terror, than from grief.

I grabbed the phone.

"What are you doing?" asked Charlie.

"Calling an ambulance," I replied, calmly.

Revenge

There were six of them in all who'd had
the beef, including Mia and Charlie. They
tumbled into the back of two ambulances,
like calves boarding a cattle-truck.

I went with them. I had to, Mia was in
such a state. None of them felt like talking,
obviously, so I tried to keep them cheerful by
chattering away. Somehow though, I found
I couldn't stop myself saying words like
"E. coli", "mad cow disease" and "poisoned".
I decided to change the subject.

"Let's hope they don't have to put you
under general anaesthetic," I said. "Danny
Murphy's cousin was given an anaesthetic

and they stole one of his kidneys and sold it to some human organ dealer." Charlie groaned and one of the girls started sobbing.

They didn't give them a general anaesthetic, so I stayed with Mia as the long rubber tubes were pushed down her throat and into her stomach. Then for just one moment, while they were pumping and Mia was sobbing and retching away, I felt rather guilty. But it was only for one moment.

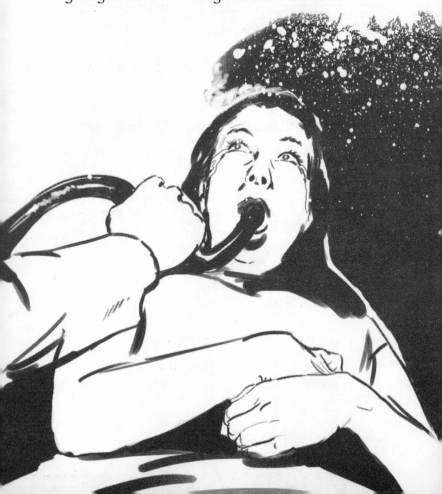

After they'd all had their stomachs pumped, everyone looked a whole lot worse than when they'd arrived. Various people's parents turned up to take them home.

Mia turned to Charlie: "You will come back with me, won't you, Charlie?" she whispered, hoarsely. The stomach tube had made her throat very sore.

"Well…" Charlie croaked. His throat was sore, too.

"Oh, thank you so much, Charlie!" I said. "We wouldn't be able to dig Jasper's grave on our own."

Charlie looked horrified. He'd imagined spending the evening with his hands around my sister's waist, rather than round the handle of a spade, digging a dog's grave in our back garden.

"Actually, I think I ought to go home. Mother's dreadfully worried about me."

Mother? What did he sound like?

Mia and I got a taxi home. She was still very weak, but she helped me to wrap poor Jasper in a blanket and drag him into the garage. When Dad got home, he would bury him in our pets' graveyard by the potato patch, where he would join Rory the rabbit, Hammy the hamster, and Roddy the rat.

I went to bed then, and fell straight to sleep. But I didn't sleep well. I kept being woken up by the sound of the toilet flushing.

When I went downstairs next morning, I found Mia tidying up the remains of the party, so that the lounge would look spotless when our parents came back. She looked terrible and kept clutching her stomach, still sore after being pumped out.

I started cooking bacon and runny fried eggs, and Mia dashed off to the bathroom.

Then the doorbell rang.

A scruffy little man, wearing thick glasses, stood on the doorstep, nervously shuffling from one foot to the other.

"Is your dad in?"

I shook my head. "He'll be back later," I said. "He's away for the weekend with Mum."

The man was wriggling and twisting like a worm. He looked back over his shoulder towards the road. His car was parked outside our house; a bright red car.

"I'm the driver of the car that ran over your dog."

"Oh…" I couldn't think of anything else to say.

"He managed to stagger back here, didn't he?"

I nodded.

"He ran out into the road, straight in front of me. I didn't have a chance. I panicked, I'm afraid and just drove off. I haven't slept a wink all night. In the cold light of day, I realised I had to do the right thing and come and tell you." He paused. "Is he… you know…?"

I nodded, again.

"I'm so, so sorry. I do hope he didn't suffer too much."

"No, no," I said, thinking of the rubber tube I'd seen stuffed down Mia's throat, and of all the texts she had sent Charlie since last night that he hadn't replied to. "Jasper didn't suffer at all."

The man nodded, sadly. Then he turned and went back to his car.

I closed the front door. Mia appeared at the top of the stairs. "Who was that?"

"Just some bloke."

"Not… Charlie…?"

"No, not Charlie," I replied. "Would you like some runny fried eggs and bacon?"

Mia dashed back into the toilet.

Or if you like, I murmured to myself with a wicked smile, I could fix you up a nice beef sandwich.

Don't Look Under the Bed

1

Griff

Lexi hit the button on the TV remote. The picture vanished in a flash, leaving the screen completely blank.

Local TV news was always so boring. Tonight, someone in the studio had been moaning about a new road being built. Then they'd cut to some dumb reporter in a muddy field surrounded by police cars, wittering on about a nutter who had escaped from a prison van. This had been followed by an item about an old woman who had taught her budgerigar to squawk the Doctor Who theme tune. Was there really nothing more important happening?

Lexi yawned. Her older sister, Natasha, was at a party and wouldn't be home until late. Her father and stepmother were away in Manchester. She was being kept company by Griff, her German shepherd dog. He had been given to her as a puppy just after her mother walked out. Griff lay flat out, fast asleep on the rug.

Lexi got up. Griff cocked an ear, half opened an eye and then went back to sleep. Lexi went out into the hall and up the wide, creaking staircase to her room. She'd never really liked this house. Her father had bought it when he had married Caroline, her stepmother.

"James, darling, it's simply divine!" Caroline had gushed. "Such an improvement on that pokey little cottage." And her father had smiled.

But Lexi had liked the "pokey little cottage" she and Natasha had lived in with their father. It had been snug and cosy. This house they lived in now was too big; too noisy. It rattled and creaked with every move you made, as if it hated you being there.

Lexi went to the window. In the night sky, dark clouds moved swiftly across the moon. They made the shadows of the old trees at the end of the garden dance eerily

on the lawn. Lexi held up her tablet and had just started to post a new message on her Facebook page, when her phone rang. She jumped. She had been jittery about answering the phone when she was alone ever since a friend had told her a true story. It was about a babysitter who was rung up by some pervert, but he was actually in the house with her!

Lexi pulled out her phone. It was only a text:

> **Rob completely LASHED! Cant drive. So no lift.**
>
> **Staying Caitlins. Sorreee!**
> **c u. Tash x**

Typical, thought Lexi, angrily. Just like Tash and her grinning boyfriend to behave so irresponsibly.

She texted back:

> **Cow!**

−2−

Sharp white teeth

It was alright for Tash, sleeping over at
Caitlin's − with Rob. She didn't have to
spend the night alone in this gloomy old
house.

Then Lexi remembered the news item
about the escaped prisoner. Her heart
skipped a beat. Hadn't there been some sort
of police warning? If there had been, she
couldn't remember what it was. She got the
local news pages up on the Internet.

And felt her mouth go dry.

The prisoner who had escaped was
described as "violent". The police were
warning members of the public "not to

approach this man". As if, thought Lexi.
There was a police photo of the escaped
prisoner. He was square-jawed, shaven
headed, with eyes as cold and hard as flint.

Lexi shivered.

She read on. The police were also advising people to lock their doors, windows and garden sheds.

He was out there, this dangerous, desperate man, and she was all alone.

Not quite all alone, though, she thought. Griff was downstairs. He might be a great, big softie with family members, but Lexi knew he had a scary bark and a ferocious growl. She guessed he could rip the flesh off your leg in one easy bite.

She went back downstairs. Griff was still asleep on the rug. She stroked his long, coarse fur.

"You're sleeping in my room tonight, Griff," she told him. "You'll see off any nasty men, won't you?" Griff stretched and yawned. Lexi saw his sharp white teeth and felt comforted.

"Come on, boy!" Lexi called. Griff followed her as she walked round the house, checking that every window was locked and every door bolted.

"The police said check your garden sheds, but I'm not going out there at this time of night. What's in there, anyway? Dad's ride-on mower? Hardly a getaway vehicle for a dangerous criminal." She couldn't get the police photo of the escaped prisoner out of her mind, though. She picked up the tattered old blanket from Griff's bed, switched off the downstairs lights, and went back upstairs to her room. Griff followed her.

Lexi put Griff's blanket just out of the way under her bed. Griff had sometimes slept under her bed before, in the old cottage, on nights when she had been particularly upset or unhappy, and was missing her mum. She changed into her PJs then peered briefly out of the window. The cloud cover was

thickening, the wind rising. It looked like a storm was brewing.

Lexi turned out the light and snuggled down.

"Night, Griff," she whispered, and putting out her hand she patted Griff's head. Griff turned his head and Lexi felt the palm of her hand being nuzzled, first by his cold, wet nose and then by the roughness of his tongue. Just knowing that Griff was so close to her gave her comfort and reassurance. It was not long before she drifted off to sleep.

A warm, wet lick

When she woke, Lexi thought it might already be morning. But as she opened her eyes she saw that there was no welcoming sunlight shining through the curtains. She turned over to look at her bedside clock; the LED display read 02.55. She put her arm down by the side of the bed. Almost immediately, she felt the palm of her hand being gently licked.

"Good boy, Griff," she whispered. "Good boy."

She lay awake, listening. As well as the usual creaking from the timbers in the old house, she thought she could make out another sound; a kind of steady, drip, drip, drip. Still, if they'd had a storm, she thought, it was probably just the rainwater dripping off the trees outside her window.

She snuggled right down under the covers, but sleep wouldn't come. "Don't worry, Lexi," she kept saying to herself, "if there's someone in the house, Griff will bark."

She still wished it was morning, though.

She heard Griff's steady breathing from under the bed, put her hand down again and received another reassuring warm, wet lick on the palm of her hand. This time it was even stronger than before.

"Thank goodness I've got you, Griff," she whispered to herself, as her eyelids closed and she drifted back to sleep.

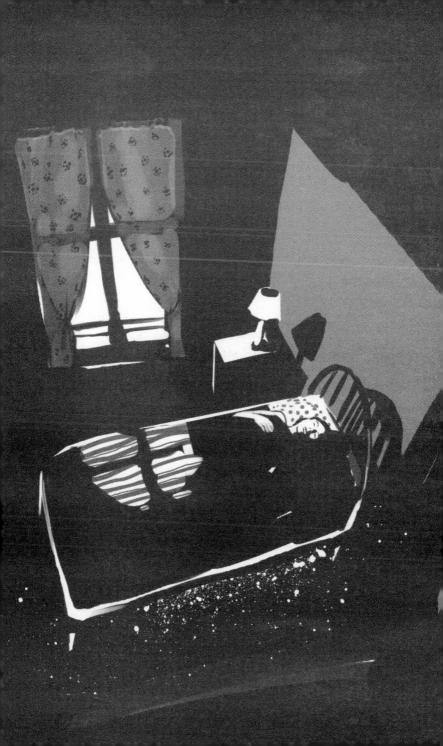

— 4 —

The blood trail

When Lexi opened her eyes again, the room was bathed in light.

Instinctively, she put her hand down by the side of the bed and waited for a friendly lick.

Nothing.

She leaned out of her bed. The blanket was there, but where was Griff? Then Lexi's eyes caught sight of a row of bright red spots on Griff's blanket. Her eyes followed the line of red patches all the way across the carpet to her bedroom door.

Lexi leapt out of bed and scurried across

to the door. Deep down she sensed that something bad had happened. Nothing could have prepared her for what she saw on the landing, though.

Scrawled across the huge gilt-framed mirror on the wall opposite, in bright red, dripping letters were the words: "humans can lick too".

Lexi screamed, and kept on screaming as her eyes followed the blood trail. The red splatters led across the landing and all the way down the stairs. She drew in great, heavy sobs and screwed up her eyes tight. She didn't want to see where the trail ended. But at the same time she needed to know what had happened. She opened her eyes and slowly, through a haze of tears, she began to walk down the stairs.

THE END....

DEADLY TALES

One book.
Two nightmares.

978 1 4451 0340 2 pb
978 1 4451 0855 1 eBook

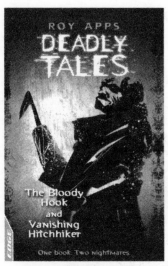

978 1 4451 0337 2 pb
978 1 4451 0852 0 eBook

978 1 4451 0341 9 pb
978 1 4451 0856 8 eBook

978 1 4451 0339 6 pb
978 1 4451 0854 4 eBook

978 1 4451 0336 5 pb
978 1 4451 0851 3 eBook

Find out more about these books and
others published by EDGE at:
www.franklinwatts.co.uk

Plus visit Roy's website for the latest
news on all his books:
www.royapps.co.uk

DEADLY TALES

TEASER

Can't wait to find out what happens in the other DEADLY TALES urban legends? Well, here's a teaser from The Hangover:

Slowly, Curtis became aware of a pain in his side; as intense and piercing as a scream. His whole body ached. He shivered. He was cold. And wet. He opened his eyes and could just make out row upon row of corrugated iron fencing reaching up to a grey, early morning sky. Somewhere, not far off, he could hear a dog barking angrily.

Curtis put out his hand and felt the rough, hard texture of a cinder track, and then something wet, like a puddle. Was he in a nightmare? He closed his eyes again, desperate to wake up. Then he opened his eyes slowly and the reality hit him like a train. The cinder track he was lying on was real; the cold and wet was real; and above all, the pain was real.

This was no nightmare. This was his morning.

✝

Dare you to read the rest in:
DEADLY TALES
The Hangover
and
Dead Man Drinking

Want to read more horror? Try iHorror by
The 2Steves, where you are the hero and
have to choose your own fate.

Fight your fear. Choose your fate.

978 1 40830 985 8 pb
978 1 40831 476 0 eBook

978 1 40830 986 5 pb
978 1 40831 477 7 eBook

978 1 40830 988 9 pb
978 1 40831 479 1 eBook

978 1 40830 987 2 pb
978 1 40831 478 4 eBook

www.orchardbooks.co.uk